This ThimbleBook belongs to:

Thimble the Fairy's Acorns & Tea
Text © 2011 Elevé Publishing
Illustrations © 2011 Sebastian Patch
All rights reserved.
Published by Elevé Publishing, Denver, CO.
Thimble the Fairy's is a trademark of Elevé Publishing.
www.eleve-publsihing.com
Printed in China. First Printing, January 2011
This book is set in 18pt. Aunt Mildred MVB - OSF

Publisher's Cataloging-in-Publication data

Fairy, Thimble the.
Acorns & tea / written by Thimble the Fairy :
illustrated by Sebastian Patch.
p. cm.
ISBN 978-0-9827304-0-9
Summary : Through her favorite rhymes, Thimble the Fairy
tells of forest friends, wishes and dreams, planting flowers,
and building fairy houses.
[1. Fairies--Fiction. 2. Fairies--Poetry. 3. Nature--Fiction.]
I. Acorns and tea. II. Patch, Sebastian.
III. Title
PZ7.F173 Ac 2010
[E]—dc22   2010929685

Acorns & Tea

Written by

Thimble the Fairy

Illustrated By

Sebastian Patch

Elevé Publishing
Denver Colorado

Little fairy rhymes...

...for little fairies.

Fairytale is old and strong
For little children dream along
Over the hills
　　The forest
　　　The sea...

...To Fairyland
  They come for tea!

Make walls of straight twigs
A skipping stone path
Grass curtains to hang
And a pond for a bath!

Make a quilt of soft leaves
A mattress of moss
A dandelion pillow
With feathers to toss!

Acorn cap bowls
Pine needle spoons
Buttercup mugs
And bee pollen food...

...And the fairies will come
  Bringing their magic to you!

9

Fairy dust in your hair
Wish upon a star...
Follow your dream
True and fair...

...Your dream will take you far!

Help the fairies
To help things grow!
Plant some wildflower seeds
You know!
Sprinkle them gently
To the ground
Singing a song
Dancing around
A little water
A little sun
When they become flowers
Our work is done!

Plant a flower
Plant a tree
So happy will
The fairies be!

Fairies dance
And fairies sing
Fairies love the bells
Ring! Ring!

...Dance!
...Sing!
...Ring!
...Ring!

This is the song
Of the fairies!

Listen for the fairies
Look!
And look!
And look!
But not too careful
They mustn't know it...
Pretend to read your book!

Sing a song each day
Out by the garden flowers...

Perhaps you'll see a Fairy Fae
Or you may sit there for hours!

Riding upon dragonfly wing
A tiny fairy once did sing
Of babbling brook
Under shady tree
That's where a fairy's
Home will be!

Upon the dragonfly
I'd love to ride!
Sailing and darting
Climbing and dropping
As if on the steepest slide!

Here comes our friend
The sun again.
The forest is refreshed!
And all the woodland
Life is blessed!

Deep in the forest
Among the tall trees
Sing all the fairies
Buzz all the bees!

When you go to the wood
And leaves CRUNCH
Beneath your feet...
The little folk
Will dance beside you!

We fairies love to swirl
And dodge the falling leaves
And then stop suddenly
Alight on a branch
And have lunch with
The squirrels...

...Acorns and tea!

Under the harvest moon
The fairies form a ring

And Sing!
  And Sing!
    And Sing!

When autumn comes
Nestle some bulbs
Gently in the soil

Near summer's end
Their work just begins

Help the fairies
Who's work is loyal

To help them blossom
When spring comes again!

Fairies love to feed the birds
The finch
The swallow
The jay...
Put some seeds upon your sill
And sing for you they may!

While you're in your house
During winter cold
Where do all the fairies go?

They're nestled down deep
Under the snow...
Dreaming of blossoms
In Spring!

Don't forget the birds!
Remember Mr. Bumblebee!

Chirp! Chirp!
        Buzz! Buzz!

Sing a song
        Dance along

See the fairies in the trees!

An acorn necklace
From a fairy

Is a gift that you should
Treasure!

She'll place it gently
'Round your neck...

...And be your friend forever.

Be good!
Be kind!
Be true!

...And the fairies will
Watch over you!

Have a most magical day!

Yours truly,

Thimble the Fairy